# #9 Lizard Loopy

# Books in the
# S.W.I.T.C.H. series

#1 Spider Stampede

#2 Fly Frenzy

#3 Grasshopper Glitch

#4 Ant Attack

#5 Crane Fly Crash

#6 Beetle Blast

#7 Frog Freakout

#8 Newt Nemesis

#9 Lizard Loopy

#10 Chameleon Chaos

#11 Turtle Terror

#12 Gecko Gladiator

#13 Anaconda Adventure

#14 Alligator Action

# #9 Lizard Loopy

## Ali Sparkes

illustrated by
### Ross Collins

MINNEAPOLIS

Text © Ali Sparkes 2012
Illustrations © Ross Collins 2012

"SWITCH: Lizard Loopy" was originally published in English in 2012. This edition is published by an arrangement with Oxford University Press.

Darby Creek
A division of Lerner Publishing Group, Inc.
241 First Avenue North
Minneapolis, MN 55401 U.S.A.

For reading levels and more invormation, look up this title at
www.lernerbooks.com

Main body text set in ITC Goudy Sans Std. 14/19.
Typeface provided by Monotype Typography.

Library of Congress Cataloging-in-Publication Data
Sparkes, Ali.
    Lizard loopy / by Ali Sparkes ; illustrated by Ross Collins.
       pages   cm. — (S.W.I.T.C.H. ; #9)
    Summary: An intruder at mad scientist's Petty Potts' house interrupts her latest experiment, trying REPTOSWITCH on twins Josh and Danny, and when they return home they find a package that sends them on a mysterious quest.
    ISBN 978–1–4677–2112–7 (lib. bdg. : alk. paper)
    ISBN 978–1–4677–2419–7 (eBook)
    [1. Ciphers—Fiction. 2. Lizards—Fiction. 3. Brothers—Fiction. 4. Twins—Fiction. 5. Science fiction.] I. Collins, Ross, illustrator. II. Title.
PZ7.S73712Liz 2014
[Fic]—dc23                                              2013019712

Manufactured in the United States of America
1 – SB – 12/31/13

For Layla

With grateful thanks to
John Buckley and Tony Gent of
Amphibian and Reptile Conservation
for their hot-blooded guidance on
S.W.I.T.C.H.'s cold-blooded reptile heroes

# Danny and Josh and Petty

Josh and Danny might be twins, but they're NOT the same. Josh loves getting his hands dirty and learning about nature. Danny thinks Josh is a nerd. Skateboarding and climbing are way cooler! And their next-door neighbor, Petty, is only interested in one thing . . . her top secret S.W.I.T.C.H. potion.

## Danny
- FULL NAME: Danny Phillips
- AGE: eight years
- HEIGHT: taller than Josh
- FAVORITE THING: skateboarding
- WORST THING: creepy-crawlies and cleaning
- AMBITION: to be a stuntman

## Josh

- FULL NAME: Josh Phillips
- AGE: eight years
- HEIGHT: taller than Danny
- FAVORITE THING: collecting insects
- WORST THING: skateboarding
- AMBITION: to be an entomologist

## Petty

- FULL NAME: Petty Hortense Potts
- AGE: none of your business
- HEIGHT: head and shoulders above every other scientist
- FAVORITE THING: S.W.I.T.C.H.ing Josh & Danny
- WORST THING: evil ex-friend Victor Crouch
- AMBITION: adoration and recognition as the world's most genius scientist (and for the government to say sorry!)

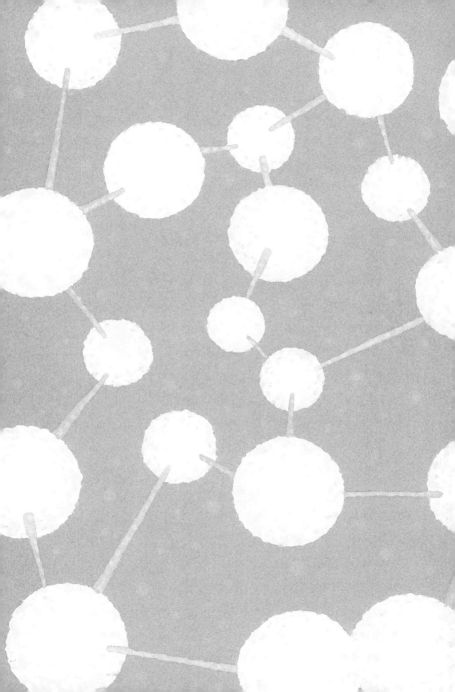

# Contents

See Ya Later                11

A Matter of Scale           25

Rolling Riddle              33

Trunk Call                  45

Wall to Wall Murder         55

T-wit                       63

Stumped                     71

Micro Mystery               81

My Spy                      87

Top Secret!                 98

Recommended Reading         100

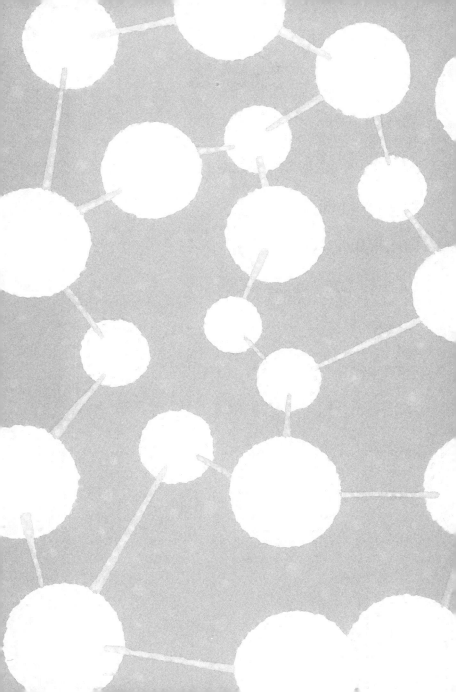

## See Ya Later

"ALLIGATOR!"

The scream echoed across the hall, filled with blood-chilling terror. Claudia Petherwaite's eyes were glassy with horror and her pink mouth was stretched wide as the scream poured out of it.

The alligator swung its snout round and located Claudia's scent. It grinned at her, taking a step closer, its dim swamp-green eyes fixing on the movement as she staggered backward toward the foldaway climbing bars. Her lunchbox fell to the floor, scattering sticks of celery and carrot across the scuffed wooden surface.

The alligator was not distracted. It smelled meat. Not veg.

"NO! NO! NO!!!" screamed Claudia Petherwaite, trying to scramble up the bars but failing because her shiny shoes were too slippery and her hands were slidey with fearful sweat.

The alligator laughed—at least it looked that way. Its snaggletoothed snout lifted and its huge mouth opened wide, getting ready to snap down on a limb.

"Shouldn't we help her?" screamed another girl, cowering by the stack of gym mats. "She's going to be eaten alive!"

"It's awful," sobbed another, just behind her. "But she was so mean to Danny in biology this morning. Maybe it's a bit harsh . . . but I—I suppose if *anyone* had to get eaten alive by an alligator . . ."

The alligator's mouth got wider still. Rows of vicious pointed teeth gleamed in the midday sun that shafted through the tall hall windows. Its stubby clawed feet dug into the wooden floor as it raised its scaly head on a thick, muscular neck. It roared and belched, and the stink of a recently dismembered gazelle wafted up toward Claudia, who was now babbling wildly, swinging on a gym rope just inches away from the ravening reptile's gaping jaws.

"I know—I know I was horrible to Danny," she shrieked. "And it was so wrong of me to say he was stupid because he couldn't spell "crysalis." I never should have laughed at him. And now, as I'm about to be eaten alive, I just wish I could say sorry to him first . . . and tell him that he's actually very clever and handsome and fabulous in e-every wa-a-ay . . . ayayaaaargh MY LEEEEEEG!"

"And then I bite her leg off," Danny said. He made a cracking and squelching noise and followed it with a gurgling scream. He rested his elbows on the gatepost and smiled happily.

"You need help," Josh said. "Professional mental help."

"What—just because I want to S.W.I.T.C.H. into an alligator and bite Claudia Petherwaite's leg off?" Danny shrugged at his twin. "Oh, come on! She's *asking* to have her leg bitten off. I bet you half the kids in school would agree with me. There was never a girl so obviously in need of losing a leg to a killer reptile. It would probably make her a much nicer person. SO—come on! Let's GO! I WANT TO BE AN ALLIGATOR!"

Josh just folded his arms and stared at him—so Danny jumped up and down and squeaked like an over-excited toddler. "Come ON! I WANT TO BE—"

Josh thwacked him on the back of the head with his hand.

"Get a grip," Josh said. "You're eight, not three!"

"But I want to be an alligator," whined Danny. "NOOOOOOOW!"

"You've acting crazy again," Josh said. "I'm taking you home." He grabbed his twin brother by the arm and yanked him up the path, away from their neighbor's scruffy old red brick house. Away from any chance of Danny becoming an alligator.

"You can just pretend for now, like you do in those embarrassing dragony questy role-play games with Scott and Zac," went on Josh, shoving Danny ahead of him down the side passage to the back garden. His twin was still so overexcited he was bouncing off the brick walls.

"They're not embarrassing. They're a laugh," chirruped Danny. "And last week I was the High Lord of Rifflescape and they were Elven Frogsprites—and I melted their heads."

Josh sighed and shook his head. "You're beyond help," he said. "There's no way you'll ever be safe as an alligator."

Back in their garden, Josh shoved Danny down by the jungle gym and called to Piddle, their dog. As Piddle (named after a habit he had when stressed) trotted over, Josh picked him up, plonked his small furry black and white body into Danny's excitable lap and said, "SIT!"

"Both of you!" he added, as Danny and Piddle tried to spring up again. They both sat, and one of them let his tongue hang out sideways.

"I'm serious, Danny!" Josh went on. He gazed across the top of the fence toward Petty Potts's back garden. Deep within its overgrown weeds and brambles stood a small, ordinary-looking wooden shed. And deep within the shed stood a small, ordinary looking door. And beyond the door nothing was ordinary ever again.

"Let me just remind you of a few things," Josh said, trying to sound like their dad. "Only a few weeks ago, we were shivering in terror about that place." He jabbed his finger across the far side of the fence. "Since then we've been nearly eaten too many times to remember! And weren't YOU the one who once said we would NEVER go back there again? Not EVER!"

"Yeah, well," Danny said, playing with Piddle's floppy ears and looking just a little bit less excitable. "That was to start with. I was freaked out. I mean, it's not every day your grumpy old next-door neighbor suddenly turns out to be a genius scientist and changes you into a spider."

Josh clambered up the climbing frame and perched on the top two bars. He stared at the roof of the ordinary shed and bit his lip. The truth was, he was very nearly as excited as Danny this time. He couldn't *wait* to try out Petty Potts's brand new S.W.I.T.C.H. spray. REPTOSWITCH! Even the name was exciting. And what it stood for. Reptile . . . Serum Which Instigates Total Cellular Hijack. He would LOVE to be a reptile for half an hour . . . BUT . . .

Josh shook his head and took a deep breath. "Danny—let's just do a checklist about how

17

the other S.W.I.T.C.H.ings have worked out, shall we?" He counted across his fingers. "ONE. SpiderSWITCH. Nearly squished by Jenny's sandal, washed down the drain, me nearly swallowed by a toad. TWO. HouseflySWITCH. Both of us nearly swatted into bluebottle jam, you wrapped up in a spider's web, me trapped in a giant booger—"

"Yeah, yeah, I know," sighed Danny. And he did know. He was usually, in fact, the more likely of the two of them to say no to any dealings with Petty Potts. For a start, while Freaky Little Bug Geek Josh loved them, Danny HATED all kinds of creepy-crawlies. He had been terrified of his own legs the whole time he was a spider. But . . . BUT . . . now that Petty had the full secret formula to make REPTOSWITCH, things were different.

There weren't nearly as many predators after reptiles, were there? They were higher up the food chain!

"THREE!" Josh went on. "GrasshopperSWITCH. Nearly splatted by a math book, nearly chewed up by a cat . . . FOUR! AntSWITCH. Turned into zombie Ant Queen-serving machines and nearly burnt alive. FIVE! Crane FlySWITCH. Almost eaten by Piddle! Nearly vacuumed to death . . . do I need to go on?"

Danny shrugged. "No. You don't. Being creepy-crawlies was 95 percent pure terror! Although the grasshopper jumping was pretty cool . . . and the housefly aerobatics . . ."

"And the great diving beetle bit . . ." Josh couldn't help smiling as he remembered. "Being able to swim under water *and* fly!"

"Being a frog at summer camp was cool too . . . apart from you—" Danny stared into Piddle's innocent fluffy face and narrowed his blue eyes accusingly—"trying to bite my legs off!"

Piddle whined guiltily.

"Point made!" Josh said.

"But don't you see? Yes—the main problem with being S.W.I.T.C.H.ed is the nearly getting eaten!" Danny said. "But *nothing* eats an alligator, does it? NOTHING!"

"You're right," came a voice from the other side of the fence. They both jumped, and Josh could see the top of Petty Potts's tweedy old hat, while Danny could make out one of her eyes behind its thick glass spectacle lens, peering through a knothole in the wood. "NOTHING eats an alligator," went on Petty. "Don't you two think it's time you came back to my lab? REPTOSWITCH is waiting."

There was a long silence in the garden, broken only by a soft whimper from Piddle. He was scared of Petty. With good reason. He got up and ran back into the house.

"Come on," went on Petty. "We're all in this together now. You are part of the S.W.I.T.C.H. Project. If you hadn't found all my missing REPTOSWITCH cubes with the secret code in them, I never would have gotten past insects, beetles, and arachnids. We've already done amphibians—and now REPTOSWITCH is perfected! It's what you've been waiting for all summer! It's finished. It works! It's time to have your reward and try it out!"

Still Josh and Danny said nothing. Petty Potts was amazing. But dangerous. She really couldn't be trusted.

"Very well," sighed Petty. "I wouldn't dream of *making* you try it. Let's just forget it. I'll go back to my lab." Her voice took on a tragic tone. "And go on with the S.W.I.T.C.H. Project alone. Don't you worry your little heads about me ever again. Maybe I'll see you at the post office someday . . . Goodbye." Petty waded across her garden, waist deep in weeds, and went into her shed. Through the door at the back. Down the secret passageway. And into her underground lab.

Danny joined Josh on the top of the jungle gym, and for a long time they stared across the fence. Danny ran his fingers through his messy blond hair and frowned. "We *want* to be alligators!" he whimpered. "Why aren't we jumping over the fence?"

"Because," Josh said, scratching his own much shorter, neater blond hair. "Whenever Petty asks us into her lab, it's like a spider inviting us into its web."

"So. We don't go," Danny said, a few seconds later. "We just . . . forget about it all."

"That would be the sensible thing," Josh said.

They stared over the fence some more.

"Let's go, then," Danny said.

They were in Petty's lab fifty-seven seconds later.

# A Matter of Scale

"We start gently," Petty said. "You've never been a reptile before, and it may be a bit of a shock."

Danny snorted. "What—like being turned into a spider *wasn't* a bit of a shock?"

"Oh, do stop harping on about that," snapped Petty, shaking a small plastic spray bottle in each hand. "You know the first time was an accident. I never intended to involve two nosy boys from next door in any of my work. If you and your dog hadn't trespassed in my lab it never would have happened at all." She beamed at them, and her gray eyes glittered behind her glasses. "And wouldn't that be a shame?"

"What kind of S.W.I.T.C.H. is in the bottles?" Josh asked, mesmerized by the green liquid sloshing around inside them.

"It's lizard," Petty said. "Two different native types. Like I said, we start gently."

"Lizard?" breathed Josh, awestruck. He adored lizards. He liked to creep up on them while they were basking in the sun and watch them for ages until they moved away like quicksilver into the grass.

"Yes," Petty said. "Now—the first time you're just going to stay right here in my lab and we'll see how it goes. As usual, it's only temporary. None of the mice have stayed S.W.I.T.C.H.ed for longer than twenty or thirty minutes so far—as with BUGSWITCH and AMPHISWITCH, I still haven't worked out a way around that."

"Just as well, probably," muttered Danny. He'd been saved from squishy, burny, or chewy death more than once by S.W.I.T.C.H. spray wearing off in the nick of time. He glanced sympathetically at the six or seven mice Petty now kept in a large cage in the corner of her lab for her experiments. They looked cheerful enough, running around their wheel and scaling the bars.

"Oooh—can't we go out in your garden for a bit?" pleaded Josh. Although it could be very

scary, one of the best things for Josh about
S.W.I.T.C.H.ing was the chance to see the natural
world from a completely different point of view.

"No! You stay put," insisted Petty. "Right—here
goes!" And she hustled them both inside a plastic
see-through tent, set up in a box shape in the
middle of her lab. "Get ready!"

Retreating through the plastic curtain, she put
her arm back in. She sprayed Josh first and then,
with a second bottle, Danny. Three seconds later,
both boys had vanished.

"Whoooo-hooo!" Josh yelled as the shimmery
plastic tent suddenly shot up and out until it was
the size of a sports hall. He stared down excitedly
at his hands—they were long-fingered and brown
and delicately scaled to the tips of their fine black
claws. Josh ran fluidly to the shaving mirror that
Petty had thoughtfully set up in the plastic tent,
tilted at just the right angle. He stared in delight
at his reflection. He was a handsome young
common lizard, with warm brown scales. Dappled
over his back was a pattern of dark brown and
light green scales. A dark line ran along the ridge

of his spine, with two pale green lines on either side. His eyes were black and almond-shaped, and his snout was pointed like a snake's.

Josh opened his mouth and poked out a gray tongue with a notch in it. Check! He knew that it wouldn't be forked like a snake's tongue. Lizards' tongues were not usually forked . . . apart from some exotic ones like monitor lizards. He turned around, admiring his long, tapering tail, which ended in a sleek point. The toes on his back feet were much longer than on his front "hands."

"I'm like a dragon!" he marveled, out loud.

"I think you'll find that I'm *more* like a dragon!" came a voice behind him, and Josh twisted around like lightning, his tail flickering behind him in an elegant S shape. He looked at Danny. There was only one reaction he could give.

"WOW!"

And then, as an afterthought . . .

"OH! WA-HA-HA-WOW!"

Danny was a thing of beauty! "You're a SAND lizard!" breathed Josh, raising his head for a better look.

Danny preened in front of the mirror. Even if he did say so himself, he was rather gorgeous—a little larger than Josh but a similar shape. What made him gleam like a jewel-encrusted treasure were the intense emerald green scales which shimmered as he moved—even as he breathed. He had a broad brown stripe down his spine scales, like Josh, but it had white diamonds running along it and a paler brown stripe on either side. He was chunkier than Josh too, and his eyes were golden with a round black pupil at the center.

"Now that," Danny said, turning in front of the shaving mirror like Josh had, "is a serious dragon look!"

"OK—you win!" Josh grinned. "I'm jealous."

"But you look cool too," shrugged Danny, still staring at his own reflection.

"So you're a sand lizard," Josh said. "And I'm a common lizard. You're rarer than I am—protected."

"Why a sand lizard?" Danny wondered. "I'm not sandy-colored. Should be an emerald lizard."

"Sand lizards leave their eggs in sand to get warmed up by the sun," Josh said. "That's why."

"Eggs," Danny said, pausing in the middle of inspecting his long green fingers. "Josh . . . please tell me I'm not a girl again. If I have to lay eggs in our sandbox, I will be mentally scarred for life."

Josh chortled. He and Danny had been S.W.I.T.C.H.ed into females twice before, once when they were ants and once when they were great diving beetles. "No—you're a guy, no question!" he assured his brother. "The females are much duller-looking. Brown—no shimmery green at all."

"Yesss!" Danny lifted his green fingers and did a high five with Josh's brown ones. "Hey—but how about you? Are you a girl?"

Josh had a good look at himself in the mirror. "Nah . . . pretty sure I'm a guy. Girl common lizards are a bit more rounded in the middle—and more yellowy."

Josh stood next to Danny, and they both peered in the mirror so intently they didn't notice a little light mist fall. "This is going to be SO cool!" grinned Danny. "And this is only the *start*! What about the BIG reptiles, eh?"

Josh opened his mouth to reply.

Then Danny suddenly head-butted him so hard he was nearly knocked out.

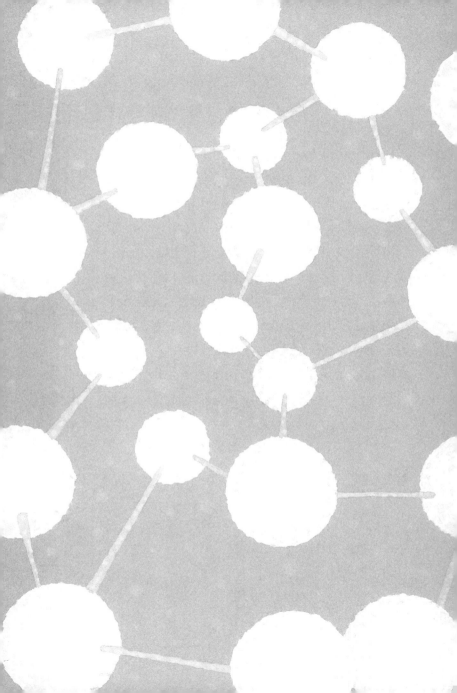

## Rolling Riddle

"A BIT of WARNING would be good!" Danny squawked as he tried to stop his nosebleed. Josh just lay on the floor, groaning and rubbing his forehead. The S.W.I.T.C.H. back had happened so fast that he and his twin had had no chance to back away from each other. They'd been smacked together at high velocity. It was like being in a minor car crash.

"SHUT UP! SHUT UP!" Petty hissed, and then Danny realized he could hear something unusual. Along with all the beeps, gurgles, and whirrs he could normally hear in Petty's lab, there was a strident beeping going on—and, somewhere outside, the shrill, nonstop clanging of a bell.

"Someone's trying to break in!" Petty said. "They've come into the house through the kitchen window." She was in her metal control booth in the corner of the lab, and as Danny and Josh staggered out of the plastic tent they could see her worried face, lit by the green glow of several computer monitors, as she hit assorted buttons and stared into various small screens.

"Should we call the police?" Josh asked. "Or . . ." He looked around him. "Maybe not . . ."

"In eight-year-old speak," Petty snapped, "well . . . duh! No need, anyway. The tripwires have been triggered. Whoever's gotten in is not going anywhere."

"Tripwires? Petty—what have you done? What have you set up with tripwires?" Josh asked, feeling very uneasy.

"Gas," Petty said with a breezy punch of a few more buttons. "Fast-acting sedative delivered at high velocity in the event of a tripwire being triggered. I have explosive canisters set up in the walls and ceilings all around the house. Unless they thought to wear a gas mask, they'll be facedown on the floor by now . . . or in the kitchen sink. Hmmm . . ." She looked slightly concerned.

"Hope they haven't drowned in the dishes. I will need to tortu—I mean, talk to them. Find out who sent them . . ."

"Come on!" Danny said, looking as freaked out as Josh felt. They raced back up the lab steps, through the wooden shed that disguised the lab entrance, and across to the house.

"Wait!" called Petty, lumbering after them like a small rhino in a skirt. "You'll need these!" She was carrying three things on elastic straps that looked very much like World War II gas masks.

Danny and Josh pulled them on. They fitted
snugly across their faces, sealing around their
noses and mouths, with dusty glass ovals across
their eyes. Petty put hers on too and unlocked the
back door to the house. As they stepped inside,
Petty made straight for the kitchen. Danny and
Josh crowded in behind her. "Aha!" they heard
her cry. But then, "Aaah . . . What?"

The kitchen window was smashed. But nobody
was on the floor or facedown in the kitchen sink.
Petty pulled off her mask. "It's all right," she said.
"The gas didn't go off."

Josh took his mask off and Danny followed, slightly fearfully in case Petty had gotten it wrong. But the kitchen smelled normal enough. Of French toast, which Petty had cooked for breakfast on her old-fashioned gas stove.

"Must've run away after smashing the window," Petty muttered. "Didn't try to get in." She looked rather disappointed, as if finding an unconscious intruder would have been the highlight of her day. "Right—off home now, boys. Before you contaminate this room. I need to run some forensic tests on the glass . . . see if I can find out who tried to get in. If he wasn't very probably dead, I would think this was the work of Victor Crouch."

Josh and Danny looked at each other. They had met Victor Crouch only once and still weren't completely sure he was the evil, backstabbing foe that Petty seemed to think he was. She was convinced that he'd tried to steal her S.W.I.T.C.H. Project work and had burnt out bits of her memory when they'd worked together in secret government laboratories.

Trouble was, Petty was so crazy about so many things it was hard to take her seriously. The Victor Crouch they had met briefly a few weeks ago had seemed pretty sinister and slightly mad . . . but then, so did Petty.

"Well," Josh said. "He would definitely be dead if we hadn't stopped you from stamping on him."

"A bad day's work!" Petty grumbled. "I wish you hadn't! He is—was—possibly still is—incredibly dangerous. To all of us! But then, if he did survive and S.W.I.T.C.H. back from being a cockroach, how come I've not heard from him again? Or maybe I just have . . ." She squinted suspiciously into the sink.

"Petty!" Danny interrupted her squinting, bouncing up and down with impatience. "Can't we have another go at LizardSWITCH?"

"Yeah!" Josh said. "We'd hardly gotten going!"

"Tomorrow," grunted Petty, peering at the broken glass now. "Go home."

"Are we safe to go through the front door?" sighed Josh. "No tripwires?"

"Plenty," Petty said. "But"—she pulled a small

silvery gadget out of her pocket and waved it at them—"I've switched the lasers off. Go home."

Grumpily, Danny and Josh let themselves out of the house and wandered back around to their own.

"She's never going to let up about Victor Crouch and all that guff," sighed Danny. "I think they're both as crazy as each other. I bet neither of them ever worked for the government at all. They probably met at bingo or something."

"Mom's going to go nuts when she sees us," Josh said. Danny's nose was still dripping blood, and Josh had a big bruise swelling up on his forehead. Mom would think they'd been in a fight.

As they reached the front gate and walked up the path, Josh got an eerie feeling—as if he and Danny were being watched. He spun around, expecting to see somebody approaching them, but nobody was there. The wind shook the leaves of the wild hedgerow across the road, but nothing seemed to be hiding in it.

"What's that?" Danny said. He was picking something up off the path. It was a small crumpled paper package. Written on it in black marker was "J & D Phillips."

"That's us." Josh peered at the package. "What's in it?"

Danny turned the small package over, just about to rip it open, when he noticed the words NOT HERE also scribbled in black on the underside. The brothers glanced about.

"End of the garden," Josh said. "In the rhododendron bush."

They ran down the side passage and through the back garden to the old sprawly rhododendron bush at the end, which had been a kind of den for them for many years. Its strong trunk and branches wiggled out in a way which created a kind of cave beneath all the waxy leaves. The earth was usually quite dry, and Mom and Dad hardly ever looked inside the cave.

In the dim light inside their hiding place, Josh and Danny unraveled the package to reveal its prize.

It was a marble.

Danny snorted. "It's some kind of joke!"

"A marble?" Josh peered at the small glass orb

in Danny's palm. It had a little ribbon of yellow color twisting through the middle and a small chip on one side. It was a perfectly ordinary marble. Not even new. They had lots like it upstairs.

"Some kid messing about," shrugged Danny.

"Wait!" Josh said, as Danny prepared to screw up the packaging the marble had arrived in. "There's a bit of paper."

There was. Words were written on it, in spidery black ink:

THIS ONE IS EMPTY. SIX OTHERS ARE NOT. WITH EACH YOU FIND, YOU MOVE CLOSER TO YOUR DESTINY. DARE YOU SEEK?

"What?" Josh screwed up his face. "Sounds like one of your lame dragony questy thingy games!"

"They are NOT lame!" Danny argued. "Hang on—there's more." He flipped over another fold in the paper and read:

CLUE 1 : WHERE THE SILENT WISE ONE SLUMBERS.

"Where the silent wise one slumbers?" echoed Josh. He thought for a while. "Oh, come on, Danny. It's got to be Scott or Zac, hasn't it? Wow! Can it be true? They've actually come out of their bedrooms and decided to set you a task in the REAL WORLD?! What will the sunlight do to their see-through skin?"

"Shut up," snapped Danny. He liked his role-play stuff as much as his skateboarding and biking. "I'm thinking . . . Silent wise one?"

"Oh, you're not taking this seriously, are you?" scoffed Josh.

Danny scrunched up his eyes and pursed his lips and nodded a few times. "Got it!" he said. "Come on! I've solved the first clue. Destiny, here we come!"

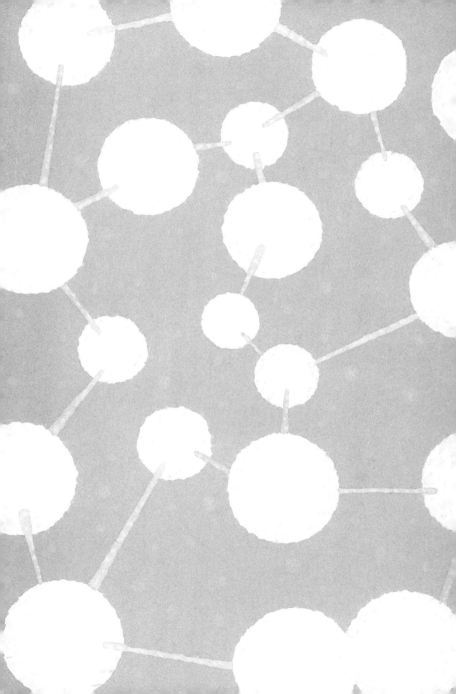

## Trunk Call

"Easy!" Danny said, getting to his feet and pushing out of the bush. "'Wise one' has got to be an owl, right?"

Josh perked up a bit. "Well—yeah, maybe. Although in reality owls aren't that clever. Of all the birds of prey they're actually the least intelli—"

"Oh, will you shut up with the nature nerding?!" Danny strode back up the garden. "Everyone calls owls wise, don't they? So it's got to be an owl. And I know where they are!"

Josh followed him down the side passage. "All right, Sherlock—where?"

"In the woods over the road, of course!" Danny said, pointing across as they arrived in the front garden. "We always hear them at night, don't we?"

"Right," Josh said. "So your destiny awaits you in the woods. Sure. Why not?" He shrugged and shook his head.

Danny didn't answer. He just shoved the note and the marble in his jeans pocket and ran out of the gate and across the quiet street. The wild hedgerow opposite had a few gaps in it and, if you pushed through, on the other side was a tangled woodland at the edge of some farmland. Danny wasn't normally keen on pushing through because of the likelihood of a spider or poisonous caterpillar falling down his neck. But today he was excited and didn't think about it. He just ran for the hedgerow and disappeared inside it.

Josh shook his head again and then followed Danny into the cool green shade on the other side. He didn't mind at all; he loved the woods. Persuading his twin to come with him was usually the problem. Danny normally preferred the pavement for his skateboard or the house for his computer games.

Some way into the wood, Danny was standing by a tall oak tree and staring up. "Look." He

pointed high. "You've always said that's got to be an owl's nest, haven't you?"

"Yeah—well—probably," Josh said. The large oval hole had formed naturally in the ancient wound of a broken off branch. It was the perfect size for a tawny owl. "But I can't imagine Zac or Scott climbing up there, can you? They get nosebleeds if they go too high on our jungle gym!"

"What if it's *not* Zac or Scott?" Danny said, his eyes shining. "What if it's not a game? It could be for real!"

"What . . . hunt the marble and find your destiny?" Josh was unimpressed. With all the amazing S.W.I.T.C.H. adventures they'd had over the past few weeks, "hunt the marble" was a bit of a comedown.

"We just have to get up there," Danny said. He was convinced he'd solved the clue and certain that something had been put up in the nest. "Give me a leg up!"

Josh frowned. "If this was earlier in the year, I wouldn't help you. She could have owlets up there—but by now they should all be fledged." He sighed, shook his head, and stooped over, leaning one shoulder against the trunk of the tree and knitting his fingers tightly into a foot sling to give his brother a boost. "You'll never do it," he warned. "It's too high and there aren't any branches."

Danny tried anyway. He was pretty fit and sporty and actually got halfway up the trunk toward the owl hole before he had to give up.

There just wasn't enough to grab hold of. He slid back down, grazing his arms on the rough bark.

"There *must* be a way!" he puffed as he landed with a thump on the soft woodland floor. He leaned against the trunk and peered at it. The bark ran like a frozen river of green and brown with a grooved pattern of deep ridges. Ants were trolling up and down it with no problem. If you were little it was a breeze!

"Waaaaiit!" breathed Danny, his eyes widening in excitement. "A lizard could get up there in seconds!"

Josh narrowed his eyes. "You're not thinking . . . ?"

"Yes! Yes, I am!" Danny bounced up and down. "We could borrow some Lizard S.W.I.T.C.H. spray, and I could get up there easily. Lizards are good at climbing, aren't they?"

"Well, yeah . . ." Josh said. "Usually . . . but . . ."

"Ah, come on! Don't be a wuss!" Danny was already running back toward the hedgerow.

"No—that's normally your job!" puffed Josh as he caught up and then shoved back through the prickly hedge. "What happened?"

"REPTOSWITCH happened!" chuckled Danny as they crossed the street and ran down the side passage to the back garden. "I was a DRAGON! Nothing eats a dragon!"

"Well, technically, you were a sand lizard," argued Josh as Danny worked the loose plank by the compost heap away from the fence post. It opened up a gap they could go through into Petty's garden. "And as for what eats them—cats, dogs, foxes . . ."

But Danny was already through the gap and running for Petty's shed. Josh paused outside. He felt uneasy again. Not just because he knew Danny was doing something he shouldn't—Petty would be furious if she found out—but because he was getting that eerie feeling again. As if they were being watched. Was the person who had left them the marble hidden away nearby, peering at them? He glanced around the garden and across to Petty's rather scruffy old house. He couldn't see any sign of anyone watching. Although Petty often warned them that government spies had her under surveillance and were keeping a top secret file on her, she was a bit bonkers and they didn't really take her seriously . . . but now . . ."No! You're turning into crazy Petty Potts! Stop it!" Josh told himself.

"Got 'em!" hissed Danny, leaping back out of the shed, patting his bulging jeans pockets. "She must be in the house, still investigating the broken window. Come on! Let's go!"

He was back through the fence, along the side passage, across the street, and back inside the wood in under a minute. Josh caught up with him as he jogged back to the oak tree.

"Look—er—Danny," he puffed, trying to keep up. "Don't you think it's a bit funny . . . Petty's window getting broken and then us finding the mystery marble? Don't you think they might be connected?"

"Nah—that's just kids messing about, breaking Petty's window," Danny said. "There were two window breaks in Florence Road last week. The Neighborhood Watch guy came around to talk to Mom about it, remember?"

"But—what if it's not kids . . . ?" Josh persisted as he and Danny arrived back at the foot of the oak. "What if Petty's been telling the truth about the government spies? I mean, we thought she'd made up Victor Crouch, but he did show up in the end, didn't he?"

"Yeah, I guess," Danny said, pulling the spray bottles out of his pockets. "But we don't know that he was a government spy, do we? Anyone can buy a walkie-talkie and act tough. How can we be sure that he wasn't just some old boyfriend from bingo who fell out with her? How can *she* be sure, with her messed up memory?"

Josh shuddered. Victor Crouch was tall and bony and had no eyebrows. He couldn't imagine Victor Crouch, with his oddly bald brow and extra long pointy nail on one little finger, being anyone's boyfriend!

"And anyway, whether he was a spy or not, she S.W.I.T.C.H.ed him into a cockroach, so that was probably the end of him," Danny said.

"Yeah, but . . . we always managed to survive. And if he did too and S.W.I.T.C.H.ed back . . ." insisted Josh.

"JOSH! You're turning into Petty!" Danny plonked the spray bottles in his twin's hand. "Now shut up and S.W.I.T.C.H. me! Use the one with S on it. That must be for sand lizard."

The other bottle had a C on it, presumably for common lizard. Petty's labeling was a bit unreliable, but this time it was correct. Three seconds later a brilliant green sand lizard shot up the oak tree. Josh marveled at the way Danny climbed the slightly slanted trunk, like shiny liquid flowing upstream. He would be sensible and wait for Danny to come back—probably with nothing—after investigating the owl hole.

Hmmm. Something about that last thought prickled at him. Owl hole. Lizard . . .

"AAAAAARGH! DANNY!!!" Josh shrieked. "DON'T GO IN THERE!"

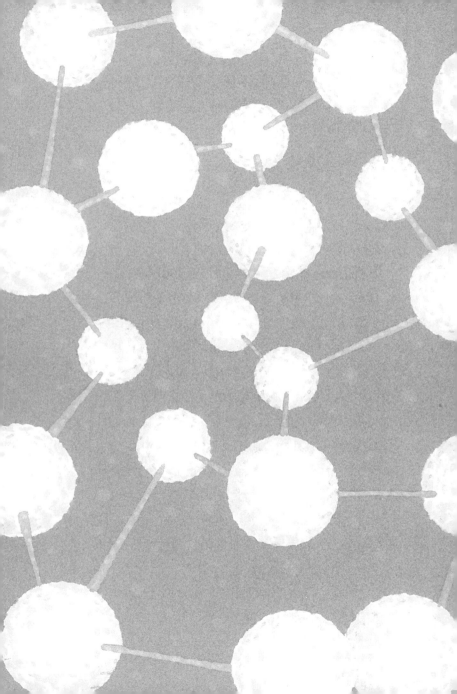

## Wall to Wall Murder

With a bolt of horror, Josh had come to his senses. There was very possibly going to be an OWL in that hole! Very likely a hungry owl. And Danny had just S.W.I.T.C.H.ed himself into a sparkly green Meals On Heels delivery!

But Danny didn't seem to have heard him. He was wriggling up the trunk at great speed, his strong lizard fingers and toes hooking effortlessly into the groovy bark, licking up a few ants as he went.

Josh groaned and shouted again, but Danny went on climbing. He was so excited about that stupid marble he was just about to offer himself up as owl food without even realizing it!

There was nothing else for it. Josh couldn't climb up after him as a boy. He looked at the bottles in his hand, picked up the C one (swiftly remembering a common lizard had better camouflage on a tree trunk) and S.W.I.T.C.H.ed himself.

Danny reached the owl hole in no time at all. Running up the tree had been amazing and much easier than the climbing wall at their summer camp. His long-fingered hands and feet, with their sharp curved claws, had anchored easily into the deep ridges winding through the bark. There were even tasty snacks along the way! Danny tried not to think about what those snacks were. They'd been great . . . he was sure they hadn't really had wriggling legs. No—they were just seeds which he'd picked up in passing by darting out his quick long tongue. Little, browny seeds. Little moving browny-black seeds with anxious faces . . . Eeeerrm . . .

But then he reached the lip of the big hole and forgot all about the snacks as his heart sped up with excitement. Whatever it was their Mystery Marble Sender wanted them to find, he was certain it was here. *Where the silent wise one slumbers . . .*

There was a strong smell coming from the
hole. A musty, sharp smell that made Danny
shiver as he clung to the curved woody lip of the
oval entrance to the chamber. His lizard sight
was good, and as his golden eyes adjusted to
the gloom, he could see that the floor of it was
covered with . . . eurgh . . . broken bits of bone
and feather in a lumpy porridge of dark gray owl
pellets and paler gray owl poo. That was one
nasty carpet.

"The carpet of death!" he muttered to himself,
and it seemed as if a horror film-style shriek went
off somewhere in the distance.

The gruesome flooring led around a corner, past a shoulder of ancient rotting wood. There was nothing that looked like a marble sitting on it. The marble must be tucked farther in. He shivered. He really didn't want to go across the carpet of death and into the inner chamber. But if he didn't all his efforts would be for nothing. Even if it was just a joke, he still wanted to get that marble.

He stepped onto the carpet. It crumbled under his front foot, sending up some unpleasant dust and a worse smell. Danny reminded himself he was a dragon (sort of) and put another foot bravely forward.

"Daaaneeeeee!" He froze. That was Josh. But he didn't sound as if he was down on the woodland floor. He was closer than that. Suddenly another lizard popped up behind him.

"Hey! You want to come in with me?" grinned Danny, very relieved. It would be much less scary going around that bit of rotting wood with his brother. He didn't tell Josh how creeped out he'd been, though.

"No! No! Danny—stop!" panted Josh, who had run up the tree at top speed.

"Why? We're here now. Might as well check it out!" Danny said.

"No—you don't understand. And I can't believe I didn't tell you this. Look—you're a lizard!" Josh was looking edgily into the hole past Danny.

"Yeah! Great, isn't it? All those insects I used to be scared of," beamed Danny. "I can eat 'em! Not that I would, of course . . . I mean . . . eeeyuw!"

Josh didn't point out the half an ant stuck to Danny's upper lip. "Yes, but you're not off the menu! I told you! Bigger things will eat you . . ."

"Yeah—you said. Cats and dogs and foxes . . . but I can't see any of those showing up here, can you? Not this high up!"

"I didn't get to the end of the list!"

"What? What else is there?" Danny said, but Josh wasn't looking at him anymore. His almond-shaped black eyes were bulging and shiny and fixed on something behind Danny. On something on the other side of the carpet of death. Something peering out from behind a screen of old trunk wood.

Something went "Keu-uu-wik!"

Before he could even scream, the talons closed around Danny—and around Josh too. And Josh knew this time it really was all over.

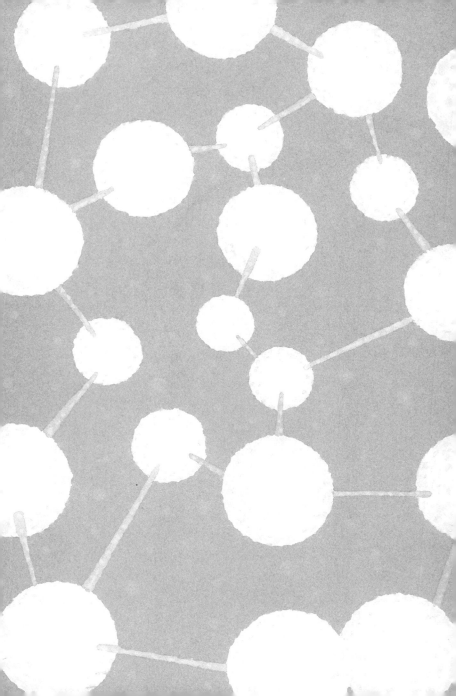

# T-wit

Josh shut his eyes, readying himself for the horrible moment when his entrails were hooked out of his belly by the small but vicious beak of the tawny owl that loomed over him. He didn't want to see that happen to Danny either. He hoped it would all be over fast.

But suddenly he felt himself swoop upward, the air whistling past his head. His eyes sprang open, and he realized he was paragliding high through the trees, the tawny wings above him making barely a sound against the air currents. "JOSH!" squeaked Danny, who was riding in the owl's other talon, his arms and legs flailing wildly. "Where's he taking us?!"

"She," corrected Josh. "She went kee-uu-wick . . . or t-wit, if you like. Females do the t-wit. Males do the t-woo."

"Does it matter?" Danny squawked. "I mean—helloooo!—certain death only seconds away and you're still being a nature nerd!"

"It could matter," yelled Josh. "If she's a mom!"

"Doesn't seem very motherly to me!" wailed Danny as their deadly pilot made a tight, stomach-flipping turn to the left, avoiding some viciously spiked hawthorn twigs by inches.

"No—but she might still be mothering her teenagers," called Josh, feeling the faintest flicker of hope. "I think she must be. That's why she didn't eat us herself. She's probably chucking some food at her kids. They're out of the nest now but still hanging around like . . . you know, like Jenny." Their teenage sister was fiercely independent . . . as long as Mom made all her meals and ironed all her clothes and drove her everywhere.

"Rii-ight." Danny gulped, now trying to keep still because the talons only tightened around his chest when he wriggled. "So we're teen munchies, then! Just a couple of cans of Pringles! How is that better?"

"Well . . ." quavered Josh as the owl swooped down and leveled out, flying low and straight with great purpose. "They might not be able to caaaaaaaaaaaaaaatch!"

The talons released, and they were both flung through the air in the direction of two young tawnies sitting side by side on the top of a battered old wooden hut beneath the trees.

Josh hit the wooden roof at high speed and rolled over and over. Even as his world spun and flipped like a rollercoaster, he was aware of the young birds leaping up and around, huge brown and cream wings flapping, curved talons out. Mom had just come back from the store.

"ROLL ON!" Danny bellowed, to his left, and Josh did. He kept tumbling over and over even as the lamp-like eyes of one of the owlets closed in on his head and a talon reached for him. Danny plunged over the edge of the roof and down into the ivy that climbed up it. Crackles, snaps, and yelps filled the air. Josh was determined to follow him when an awful, hot, stabbing pain shot through his tail. The owl's talon had pierced right through and into the wood underneath it, pinning him to his doom.

"GETOFFME! GETOFFME!" Josh shrieked and threw himself wildly from side to side, but the young owl had him now and was peering at him curiously, taking its time. It tilted its terrifyingly beautiful face to one side and gazed at him through two huge, unblinking dark orbs.

"Let me have a bit," said the other young owl.

"You had yours," said the first.

"Nah—it went over the back," complained the other.

"Not my fault," said the first. And it lowered its beak to Josh's poor soft belly.

SNAP! Josh suddenly pinged away, freed from the talon spike, and was over the edge of the old hut and tumbling down through the ivy in half a second. The owl gave a cry of annoyance. "See! Now you know how it feels," said the other one.

They didn't try to go after their departed meal. The ivy and brambles at the foot of the old hut were too thick to get through. As Josh came to rest on the lowest tangle of undergrowth, he couldn't even speak. The wind had been knocked out of him.

"Josh! Jo-o-oosh!" Suddenly Danny was scrambling across to him. "I thought you were a goner that time! I really did." He sniffed. "How did you get away?"

"I—I don't know . . ." Josh croaked. He was lying on his back exposing his pale belly, which had so nearly been a warm, skin-crusted casserole for owl-kind. His tail hurt, strangely, quite high up, considering the talon had gone through the bottom half.

"Whoa—bro! I think you should take a look at this," murmured Danny, pulling Josh up by his shoulder. Danny pointed a shaking green finger at the bottom end of his brother.

Josh's tail was now just a stump.

## Stumped

"Eeeugh," shuddered Danny. The stump was bleeding.

Josh flipped himself upright and curled what was left of his tail around to scrutinize it. In fact it wasn't bleeding that much—just across the wound; not spurting all over the place like it would be if someone cut his leg off. Josh couldn't see any snapped-off tailbone amid the goo. Instead of gaping in horror, though, he grinned. "That is SO amazing!" he said. "I'd forgotten about that!"

"What?" Danny was still looking revolted and a little panicky. "I don't know why you're so chirpy. What if you S.W.I.T.C.H. back and find you've lost a foot or something?"

"Nah, won't happen," Josh said. "A toenail maybe. You know what? I did that deliberately!"

He pointed proudly at the stump, which had stopped bleeding altogether now and was already scabbing over.

"What—chopped your own tail off? Are you nuts?" spluttered Danny.

"Chop—no—detach, yes! Don't you remember? Lizards shed their tails if they get in a panic! And it doesn't get much more panicky than being owly din-dins. My tail detached! I bet it's still up there wriggling about now!" He chuckled, even though he did feel a little bit dizzy at the thought of it. "They wriggle on their own for ages after they've dropped off, to distract the predator from the rest of the lizard while it runs away."

"That is quite cool," Danny admitted. "As long as you aren't missing a limb when we get back to human form."

"Nah," Josh said again. "Remember when we were crane flies? We lost lots of legs between us, didn't we? And we still came back to normal . . . well, apart from wanting to headbutt hot lightbulbs . . ."

"So now what?" Danny looked around anxiously. "A fox could get in here, maybe . . ."

"More likely a weasel," Josh said. "We're not safe. We never are while we're S.W.I.T.C.H.ed. I can't believe we did this again."

"Well, next time we'll just stay put in Petty's lab," Danny said. "So we can S.W.I.T.C.H. and come back to normal without a scratch."

Suddenly Danny exploded out of the brambles—as a full-sized human eight-year-old. He got a lot of scratches.

Thud! Crackle! Rip! Josh joined him a few seconds later with a howl of pain. The brambles had scraped red wounds across their cheeks and foreheads and arms. They both looked as if they'd been in a serious fight.

Two young owls took off in haste from the little wooden hut behind them. Danny went up on tiptoes, peered over the low roof, and then gave a squawk of revolted delight. "Looook!" he said. "Your tail!" A bloodied bit of scaly tail-tip was indeed writhing back and forth on the roof. "That is beyond creepy!" Danny said.

"Could've been worse," muttered Josh, checking his limbs and finding them all intact. "Now—can we go home please?" He headed off back towards the oak to collect the S.W.I.T.C.H. spray bottles.

"But what about the marble?!" insisted Danny, following him. "We still haven't found it!"

"Well, if you think I'm going back in that owl nest again, you're off your head!" snapped Josh. "I've got a whole bag of marbles at home. I don't need any more."

"But . . . our destiny!" whimpered Danny.

"Don't you think it's exciting enough?" demanded Josh. "We're going to help Petty Potts reveal

S.W.I.T.C.H. to the world someday soon. We'll be famous! The only kids on the planet who've been insects and spiders and frogs and newts—and now lizards. We've even TALKED to real animals! Isn't that a pretty cool destiny already?"

"I suppose . . ." huffed Danny. "I just hate not being able to solve the riddle . . . Where the silent wise one slumbers . . . We found it! We found the silent wise one in its bedroom . . . but we didn't get to look for the marble."

Josh suddenly stopped and turned to Danny. He laughed and clapped his hand to his scratched and bleeding forehead. "We were looking in the wrong place anyway, Danny!" he chortled.

"What? We weren't! It was the right place, I know it!"

"No." Josh shook his head as he walked another yard and collected the S.W.I.T.C.H. spray bottles from under the oak tree. Up in the hole they could see the female owl back in her roost, sitting very still with her eyes half-closed. "She's not silent. Nor is a male. They go *t-wit—t-woo* all the time, remember?"

"Don't remind me," shuddered Danny. "I'll get the heebies every time I hear it from now on."

"But what you won't hear," went on Josh, "is a barn owl. I mean, they do make noises—they can screech and hiss—but 95 percent of the time they are completely silent. They don't go *t-wit* or *t-woo*. They are the quietest bird on the wing. That's why they can hunt in daylight."

"But the tawnies were out in daylight," pointed out Danny.

"Just roosting, half asleep," Josh said. "Not hunting. I mean, Tawny Mom didn't hunt us, did she? She only woke up when we showed up, all delicious and defenseless. No—tawnies roost in trees and other places, having a bit of a doze through the day—but they usually only hunt at night. Barn owls hunt at dawn and dusk and sometimes even in broad daylight. Reeeeallly silently. Your marble . . ."

"Our marble," Danny corrected. "The package and the message were for both of us!"

"OK—our marble," Josh said, turning back across the wood and walking fast, "is in a barn owl nest. And I know exactly where to find one. I put it up myself."

"You did what?" asked Danny, scooting up behind his brother.

"I went out on a Wild Things nature day last summer, and we put up bat boxes and bird boxes. I put up a barn owl box in Farmer Coggins's barn. Just the other side of this wood. I even know where the ladder is kept for checking the box. I can undo the top. We don't have to S.W.I.T.C.H. again."

They reached the old barn ten minutes later. In the gable at one end, as Josh had said, was a stout wooden nesting box. And around the corner of the barn, behind some bales of hay and a couple of old steel drums, stood a wooden ladder. Josh eyed the ladder and then looked up at the box with a frown. "I really shouldn't be doing this, you know," he said.

"Of course you should!" argued Danny.

"It's not good to disturb wildlife," Josh said.

"Josh!" snapped Danny. "Wildlife has *more* than disturbed *me* today!"

Josh grinned. "True!" he said. "And there won't be any babies . . . Hold it steady for me!" He set up the ladder under the owl box. Danny did, and soon Josh was detaching the top of the box. A sudden flurry of white and golden feathers rocked him back on the step. The barn owl was high in the air in three seconds. Josh gazed after it, enthralled for a moment, and then reached into the box. He felt about, grimacing, and then replaced the lid and came back down the ladder. "Yuck!" he said. "It stinks in there!"

And then he held out his hand. In it, with some gray goo and bits of feather stuck to one side, was a marble.

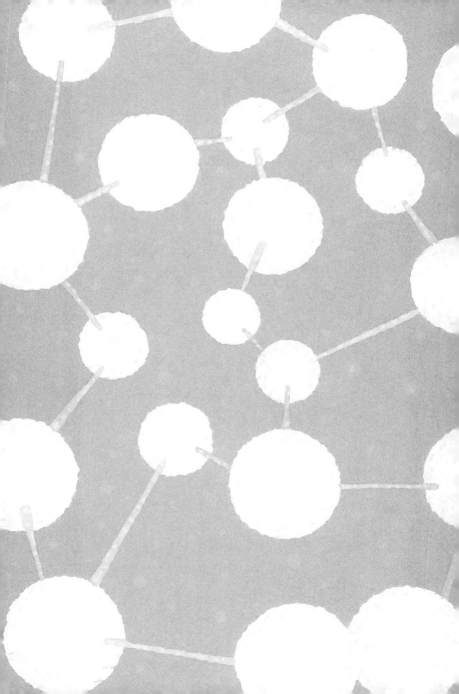

## Micro Mystery

"Keep it still!" Josh said, glaring impatiently up at Danny. "I'll never see anything if you keep waving it about!" He bent his head back to the lens of the microscope that he'd placed on the air hockey table and peered again at the magnified marble, held between Danny's magnified thumb and forefinger.

On the way back through the woods, they'd squinted at the small glass orb time and time again, trying hard to work out if it was anything but a perfectly ordinary marble. The ribbon of colored glass threading through its core was blue this time, but aside from that it seemed very unexciting—considering they'd both nearly been eaten alive trying to find it.

But Danny was convinced it was something

very important to their "destiny," so Josh dug out his microscope as soon as they got back to their bedroom.

"Well, it's very clear glass," he murmured as he looked again. "Better quality glass than my normal marbles, I think." He'd studied lots of his things under his microscope over the years. "But . . . hang on! Hang on, hang on! Hang . . . on!"

"I am hanging on!" Danny said. "What can you see? What is it?"

Josh raised his eyes to Danny, one of them a little pink from pressing against the viewer. "We've seen this before," he breathed. "Look!" He took over the marble-holding duty, pinning the glass orb steadily to the plate beneath the microscope, and waved Danny in to look.

As his eye adjusted, Danny drew in a shocked breath. Inside the blue ribbon of glass within the orb was something else . . . There was a holographic image right inside the glass. It looked like a bat. And there were symbols . . . old, strange symbols too. "It's a hologram and symbols—like in Petty's REPTOSWITCH cubes!" he gasped.

"The same! It must be another bit of S.W.I.T.C.H. code!"

"You don't think Petty set this up, do you?" Josh asked, sitting back on the bed and rubbing his tired, sore forehead. "Maybe she sent us the first marble and the message . . . just so that we would get the S.W.I.T.C.H. spray and try out being reptiles in the wild after all."

"But that doesn't make sense," Danny said. "She already knew we wanted to S.W.I.T.C.H. this time. She didn't need to trick us into it. And she was the one who told us not to go outside. No . . . this isn't Petty."

"But it's someone who knows about S.W.I.T.C.H.," Josh said. "Because those symbols in that marble are just the same as the symbols Petty uses for the BUGSWITCH and REPTOSWITCH codes."

"Check this one, too," Danny said, holding out the yellow-centered marble.

Josh did, but he soon shook his head. "No—it's ordinary. The note said it would be."

Danny read the note again. **THIS ONE IS EMPTY. SIX OTHERS ARE NOT. WITH EACH YOU FIND, YOU MOVE CLOSER TO YOUR DESTINY. DARE YOU SEEK?**

"Yep," Josh said. "Whoever sent this knew what they were doing . . . and they knew us too. Knew we would go and search . . . even knew where we would look. And I think we can rule out Scott and Zac now."

"The question is," Danny said, holding up the blue marble, "why? If someone else has code for a S.W.I.T.C.H. formula, why give it to us?"

Josh stared at the marble too. Then he nodded firmly. "It's time to tell Petty."

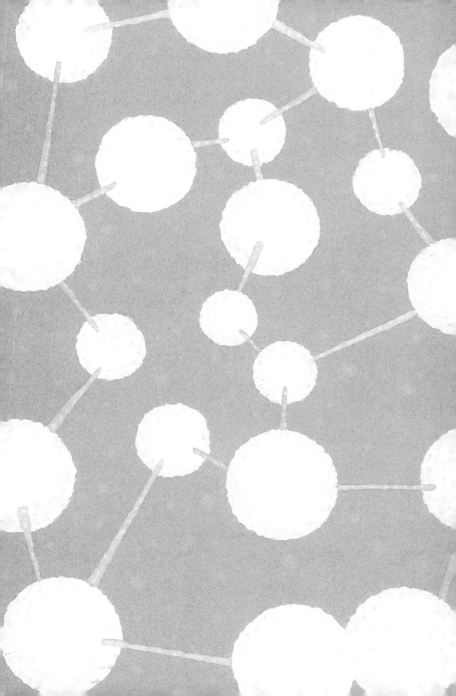

# My Spy

Somebody was replacing the glass in the kitchen window when they went round to Petty's house. A man in brown overalls stood in the side passage, pressing a new pane into the soft putty all around the frame.

"Careful now, young man!" Petty's voice rang out from the kitchen. "That's very expensive glass!"

"It's all right, love," the man said. "I know what I'm doing."

"Josh! Danny!" Petty called, spotting them loitering in the side passage. "Come through. I need to talk to you both!"

"Yeah—we need to talk to you too," Danny said. They squeezed past the glazier and went into Petty's wild back garden.

"First," Josh said, as they walked toward the

shed, "we're sorry, but we borrowed some of this."
He handed back the S.W.I.T.C.H. spray bottles.

Petty stared at them, surprised. "You stole them from my lab?!"

"No—we borrowed them," Josh said.

Petty glared at them both and then shook her head. "It doesn't matter," she said. "I'm going to have to pack up the lab and move away anyhow."

"What?!" Josh and Danny said, coming to a shocked halt.

"I'm being spied on here—I know it," Petty said, lowering her voice and looking around the garden suspiciously. "And it's just a matter of time before my secret lab is discovered. I'm going to have to find a new location."

"But . . . what about us?" Danny was appalled. Just when things had started to get less scary and more exciting! Just when he could be a snake or a crocodile or something . . . Petty Potts was leaving?

"You can't go!" Josh said. "You can't!"

"And why not?" sniffed Petty. "Most of the time you think I'm just trying to kill you anyway. Surely it will be a relief to have a normal life again, without me around."

Danny was just about to protest and show her the marble, when Josh grabbed his arm and gave him a sideways look, warning him to keep quiet.

"Well . . . if that's what you're really going to do, we can't stop you," he said. "We're just kids, aren't we? What do we know?"

"Now don't be petulant, Joshua," Petty said. "It doesn't suit you. I didn't say I would never write—or phone. I might even be able to invite you to my new lab as soon as I've built it. But it would be dangerous . . ."

"Petty—wherever you are is dangerous," Danny said.

"True," nodded Petty. "With great genius comes great peril. Anyway—I'm not going immediately. I need to find a new place first—and in the meantime I must set up more traps and tripwires all around the house. So you won't be able to pop in just like that—not unless you want to get burnt to a crisp in my hallway. I'll give you a secret knock so I know it's you. You mark my words . . ." She glared around again, and her top lip twitched three times. "They're after me! They're after me and my genius brain and they'll never stop trying to get it! Never! NEVER!" She froze, peering away into the distance, pointing and twitching occasionally.

"OK—see you later, you mad muppet," Josh muttered, dragging Danny away by the arm. "She's gone off to Bonkersville again," he muttered to his brother. "I don't think we should tell her about Mystery Marble Man right now—she'll be even worse!"

Back in their house, there was no chance to relax. Mom saw the state of their faces and bare arms and freaked out. "What happened to you both? Did you get in a fight with a bunch of rabid cats?!" she asked, staring at them in horror. There was also the dried blood in Danny's nose and the big green bruise on Josh's forehead from the head-butting incident back in Petty's lab earlier that day.

"No—we just fell into some brambles over in the woods," Josh said, quite truthfully.

"I see," Mom said. She sat them both down in the front room and dabbed at Danny's forehead with antiseptic on a cotton ball, making him wince.

"We nearly had our entrails ripped out by two giant tawny owls," added Danny, equally truthfully.

"Yes, dear, of course you did," Mom said, raising an eyebrow.

"Josh only got away because his tail snapped off," went on Danny.

Mom laughed. "You two! Such imaginations!"

Piddle came running in, his own little tail at full wag. He ran around Josh's and Danny's legs as if he was trying to round them up. He seemed rather excited.

"What is it, Piddle?" asked Josh, dropping to his knees and rubbing the little dog's black and white head.

Mom went off to get some more cotton balls. Danny knelt down next to Piddle too. He and Josh were very fond of Piddle, even if he *had* tried to eat them several times now.

"Danny!" hissed Josh. "Look!" There was something tucked into Piddle's red leather collar. A small, rolled-up bit of paper. Josh shoved it into his pocket as Mom came back, brandishing more cotton balls.

They had to wait until their wounds had been
thoroughly and painfully dabbed, and then they
went out into the garden, Piddle dancing excitedly
at their heels, to see what was in the rolled-up bit
of paper. They ran back into the rhododendron
bush to be sure they weren't seen.

"Piddle! Sit!" Danny commanded, and Piddle
did . . . mostly. His tail was wagging so hard it was
making his shaggy bottom slide from side to side.

Josh unrolled the bit of paper and saw the same
spidery writing on it. A few words had been
written in pencil:

I AM IMPRESSED. THE FULL MAMMAL
CODE . . . AND YOUR DESTINY . . . MOVES
CLOSER. AWAIT YOUR NEXT CLUE.

The brothers let out identical long breaths and stared at each other.

"Hang on—there's more . . ." Danny said, unfolding the bottom of the paper, **BREAD. COFFEE. WART REMOVER. DENTAL FLOSS.**

"Um . . . that's probably just a shopping list," Danny said. "But we're on another S.W.I.T.C.H. mission, aren't we?" His eyes sparkled with excitement. "Like when we hunted for the code hidden in the REPTOSWITCH cubes. We found all the cubes for Petty for that—but now there's a brand new MAMMALSWITCH code. Someone wants us to find it."

"But who?" murmured Josh.

"Someone with warts and good dental hygiene," guessed Danny.

"Well that's the answer! We must check the bare feet and gums of every stranger we meet!" Josh said. "But, seriously, Danny—they must be watching us. That's creepy. And maybe dangerous . . ."

"More dangerous than the last few months with Petty?" Danny asked.

Josh shrugged. "Um . . . actually, no. I *was* nearly eaten by a toad, wasn't I?"

"And I was nearly eaten by Piddle!" Danny grinned. Piddle grinned too and wagged his tail.

"Sooo," Josh said, rubbing Piddle's ears. "We keep the marble safe and talk to Petty tomorrow when she's calmed down a bit. Until then . . . let's just act normal. Or . . ." He got up and went down the garden, through the side passage and out to the front. Danny and Piddle arrived close behind him. Josh waved to the empty street and called out, "Hello, Mystery Marble Man!"

Nothing moved other than a few leaves blowing along the pavement.

"Or woman," Danny said. "Anyway, they've probably gone home now. And speaking of . . . I can smell sponge cake. Mom's baking!"

The boys looked at each other, burst out laughing, and turned and ran indoors to beg some cake off Mom.

But Piddle paused. He stared across the road. His fur began to bristle, and he let out a little whine.

And the Mystery Marble Person smiled, chuckled silently—and went home.

# Top Secret!

## For Petty Potts's Eyes Only!!

### DIARY ENTRY 641.3

### SUBJECT: THEY'RE CLOSING IN

WHAT A DAY! It started brilliantly. Josh and Danny S.W.I.T.C.H.ed into perfect specimens of a common lizard and a sand lizard—and back again—without any ill effects. REPTOSWITCH is working perfectly! But there wasn't much time for jubilation, because the alarm was triggered back in the house. Somebody broke the kitchen window, although they didn't get in, I'm glad to say. If they had, of course, I would be interrogating them right now! Electrodes would be involved.

Sometimes I can feel the shadow of Victor Crouch over me. But surely he's dead? I turned him into a cockroach, and he was quite unprepared for that—so he surely got eaten by the first blackbird or toad he encountered. And I've heard nothing more from him since, so he must be gone. Or maybe he's alive and well and just tormenting me! I just don't know.

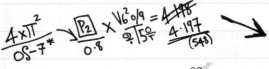

But whether it's Victor or Victor's ghost or a brand new Victor clone—they're out to get me. I know it! And maybe out to get Josh and Danny too—although surely the government can't believe that I would involve two eight-year-olds in my work? That was the brilliance of the idea! Nobody would ever believe anything Josh or Danny said.

Anyway, it pains me, but I am seriously going to have to look for a new location for my laboratory. The shed and the underground shelter are just not secure enough.

Maybe I can still smuggle Josh and Danny out to the new lab with me sometimes—they are SO useful. And I did want to reward them by letting them try out all my REPTOSWITCH sprays. I know I can work up from lizard—all the way up to . . . alligator!

And perhaps one day I will remember whether I got as far as mammals. I feel certain that somewhere in my burnt-out memory there is a clue to MAMMALSWITCH. I don't remember making any cubes, though . . . perhaps I never did.

But for now there is plenty to get on with on the REPTOSWITCH phase. Next . . . something bug-eyed and creepy with brilliant camouflage . . . chameleons, I think!

# Recommended Reading

**BOOKS**

Want to brush up on your reptile and amphibian knowledge? Here's a list of books dedicated to slithering and hopping creatures.

Johnson, Jinny. *Animal Planet™ Wild World: An Encyclopedia of Animals*. Minneapolis: Millbrook Press, 2013.

McCarthy, Colin. *Reptile*. DK Eyewitness Books. New York: DK Publishing, 2012.

Parker, Steve. *Pond & River*. DK Eyewitness Books. New York: DK Publishing, 2011.

## WEBSITES

Find out more about nature and wildlife using the websites below.

### San Diego Zoo Kids

http://kids.sandiegozoo.org/animals

Curious to learn more about some of the coolest-looking reptiles and amphibians? This website has lots of information and stunning pictures of some of Earth's most interesting creatures.

### National Geographic Kids

http://kids.nationalgeographic.com/kids/

Go to this website to watch videos and read facts about your favorite reptiles and amphibians.

### US Fish & Wildlife Service

http://www.nwf.org/wildlife/wildlife-library/amphibians-reptiles-and-fish.aspx

Want some tips to help you look for wildlife in your own neighborhood? Learn how to identify some slimy creatures and some scaly ones as well.

# CHECK OUT ALL OF THE

Spider Stampede

Ant Attack

Fly Frenzy

Crane Fly Crash

Grasshopper Glitch

Beetle Blast

 **TITLES!**

Frog Freakout

Newt Nemesis

Lizard Loopy

Chameleon Chaos

Turtle Terror

Gecko Gladiator

Anaconda Adventure

Alligator Action

## About the Author

Ali Sparkes grew up in the woods of Hampshire, England. Well—not in the sense that she was raised by foxes after being abandoned as a baby. She had parents, OK? Human parents. But they used to let her run wild in the woods. But not wild as in "grunting and covered in mud and eating raw hedgehog." Anyway, during her fun days in the woods, she once took home a muddy frog in a bucket, planning to clean it up nicely and keep it as a pet. But her mom made her take it back. The frog agreed with her mom.

Ali now lives in Southampton with her husband and two teenage sons and a very small garden pond, which has never yet attracted any frogspawn or even half a newt. Ali is trying not to take this personally.

## About the Illustrator

Ross Collins's more than eighty picture books and books for young readers have appeared in print around the world. He lives in Scotland and, in his spare time, enjoys leaning backward precariously in his chair.